ABBE
Regional Library System

On the night your momma told me she was having you I was so excited I couldn't sleep! When you were born, the whole family couldn't sleep we were all so anxious to meet you. Now sometimes at night YOU can't sleep and so we whisper stories to you about a great, brown bear. Welcome to the world, dearest granddaughter. You are so very loved. —K. W. (a.k.a. Grandma)

To Jacob —J. C.

THE BEAR BOOKS
MARGARET K. McELDERRY BOOKS
An imprint of Simon & Schuster Children's Publishing Division
1230 Avenue of the Americas, New York, New York 10020

Book design by Lauren Rille
The text for this book was set in Adobe Caslon.
The illustrations for this book were rendered in acrylic paint.
Manufactured in China
0818 SCP
First Edition
2 4 6 8 10 9 7 5 3 1
Library of Congress Cataloging-in-Publication Data
Names: Wilson, Karma, author. | Chapman, Jane, 1970– illustrator.
Title: Bear can't sleep / Karma Wilson ; illustrated by Jane Chapman.
Other titles: Bear cannot sleep
Description: New York : Margaret K. McElderry Books, [2018] | Summary: "It's time for Bear to hibernate but he can't sleep, so his friends all band together to help"— Provided by publisher.
Identifiers: LCCN 2017007066 (print) | LCCN 2017033627 (eBook) | ISBN 9781481459730 (hardcover) | ISBN 9781481459747 (eBook)
Subjects: | CYAC: Stories in rhyme. | Bedtime—Fiction. | Bears—Fiction. | Friendship—Fiction. | Animals—Fiction.
Classification: LCC PZ8.3.W6976 (ebook) | LCC PZ8.3.W6976 Ban 2018 (print) | DDC [E]—dc23
LC record available at https://lccn.loc.gov/2017007066

Bear Can't Sleep

Karma Wilson

illustrations by Jane Chapman

MARGARET K. MCELDERRY BOOKS
New York London Toronto Sydney New Delhi

In his home in the forest,
while the cold wind blows,
Bear snuggles in his quilt
from his nose to his toes.

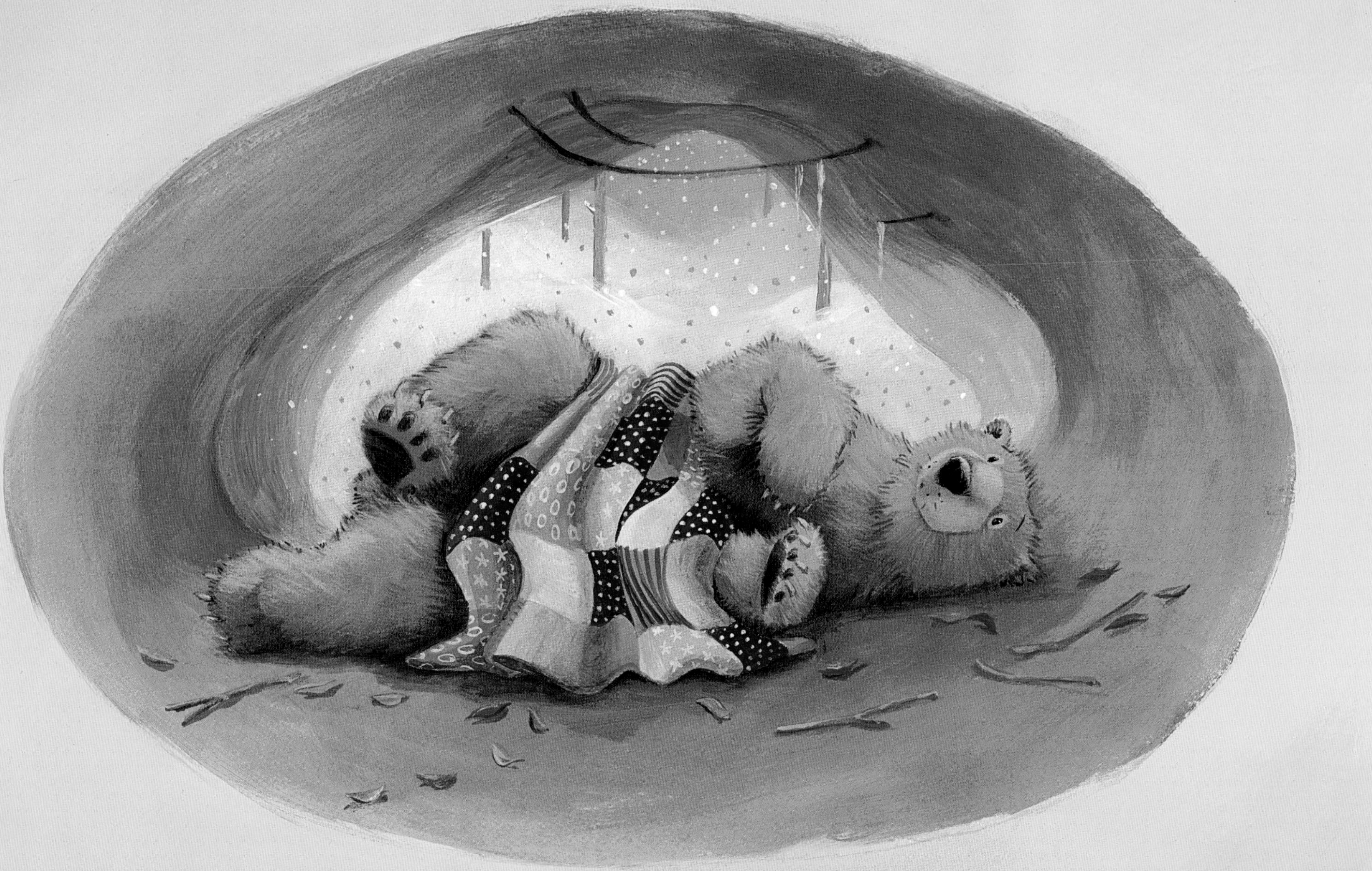

While the snowflakes fall
and the drifts pile high,

Bear tosses and he turns;
Bear moans and he sighs.

He stares at the wall; he's not tired at all.

And the bear

can't

sleep!

Pitter-pat, tiptoe.
Mouse scurries in the lair
to check on the fire
for his good friend Bear.

"Oh, Bear," Mouse squeaks,
"you are up too late.
It is winter in the woods,
and bears hibernate!"

Mouse frets—"Dear me!"—
while he brews mint tea.

And the bear

can't

sleep!

Bear is counting sheep—
"One, two, three, four . . ."—
when Badger and Hare tumble
in through the door!

"Ho, Mouse!" says Hare.
"We were just out walking.
Bear should be asleep,
but we both heard him talking!"

Bear snuggles down deep
in a sad, furry heap.

But he still
can't
sleep.

Mouse turns down the lamp.
Badger builds the fire up.
Hare pours warm milk
into Bear's tin cup.

Then Gopher and Mole
tunnel up to the lair.
Mole frets and he fusses.
"It is bedtime for bears!"

The cold wind blows
while the firelight glows.

But the bear
can't
sleep!

Wren, Owl, and Raven
flitter-flutter inside
to find Bear awake
with his eyes open wide!

Wren hops to and fro.
"What else is there to try?
A song to make him sleepy?"
So they sing a lullaby.

All gathered in the lair,
they hum along for Bear.

But he still
can't
sleep!

"I'm awake!" roars Bear.
"And that's all there is to it!
I have tried to fall asleep,
but I just can't do it!

“I’m bored, bored, bored . . .

". . . so I'll spin you all a tale.
Once upon a time
in the Strawberry Vale . . ."

The friends huddle in
as the story begins . . .

. . . since the bear
can't
sleep!

Bear tells a story
he has never told before!

But just before the end . . .

. . . there comes
a rumbling snore.

When the sun peeks up
on a bright, new dawn,
the friends can't sleep . . .

but the bear
snores
on!